NORTH OF THE HEART

A collection of poetry and prose

Anne Saddler
aka Grey Hen With A Pen

Amethyst Press

Copyright © 2020 Anne Saddler aka Grey Hen With A Pen

All rights reserved

No part of this book may be reproduced, or stored in a retrieval system, or transmitted in any form or by any means, electronic, mechanical, photocopying, recording, or otherwise, without express written permission of the publisher.

ISBN-13: 9798633807318

Cover design by: Art Painter
Library of Congress Control Number: 2018675309
Printed in the United States of America

'Every accomplishment starts with the decision to try.'

AUTHOR UNKNOWN

CONTENTS

Title Page
Copyright
Epigraph
FAMILY Ties — 1
Her Life — 3
Anne Saddler — 4
Pilgrimage To The Past — 5
The Maiden Voyage Of HMS Patia — 9
He Makes Her Toast — 12
My Grandma's House — 13
The Memories I Never Had — 15
Letter to my Granny — 17

Haiku Chain: FOR LOST CHILDREN — 21
She Had Blue Hair — 24
Love Poem To A 21st Century Woman — 25
The Photograph — 27

The Death of Beauty	29
Vincent's Irises	33
The Sword Of Truth	34
Megalith	37
The Argument	38
The Misunderstanding	39
Redundant	40
About The Author	45

FAMILY TIES

HER LIFE

Painted In Words

ANNE SADDLER

This is how she lived her life:

First, as a daughter, then as a wife.

PILGRIMAGE TO THE PAST

As I slowly rewind the video of my life/ memories begin to rattle around my brain as marbles in a pin-ball machine/their white noise demands a visual balance/black words scratched onto smooth, white wove paper/excavating old bones/ mark-making with indelible ink the discoveries/celebrating, delighting, groaning, ignoring.

The pen nib follows the roman-road of lineage/ curating and editing our shared mythical framework/my presence an intrusion/the heavy sweetness of decay unsettling/I am alone in lost landscapes/relegated to barren spaces/ untangling the knottiness of your existence.

There are many sunken places from whence the dead call/they whisper to the future from haunted landscapes/unmarked graves in an antique land of undiscovered treasures/ God's Own Country/the backbone of England, home/am I a tourist or a traveller in this terra incognita?

I journey through time instead of place/a curious outsider, snooping in archives for a scandal to make a story/reimagining lives/fleshing out testimony/exorcising demons/the dead, the only reliable keepers of secrets/the characters, phantoms who have haunted me all my life/faces looking upward in eternal slumber surrender their stories/psychic fingerprints scream guilty as charged/no fake news here.

I sit awhile amongst the ghosts/sense no connection/I should know them/I try to find excuses for their behaviour but my imagination won't allow it/I am biased by an innate moral standing born of my time/ it is a meeting of unequal worlds/there is no shared culture/no avenue of understanding/ I am the protagonist in this story/raising the dead/stirring up old troubles.

The river of ink records the sacred union of family ties which loved and reproved/ tethered and smothered/indissoluble bonds of shared genes and shared histories/frayed now by secrets and longings, madness and melancholia, match-makings and heart-breakings/stories that punch the gut and wrench the heart/footprints in a snow long melted.

These people, and the events that shaped me/
they colour my shadowed silhouette with
muted hues/purple moorland heathers/ flat
green dales/grey city walls/shy blues and
white roses/all viewed through mood-ring
eyes/eyes that won't lie, that can't keep
secrets or mask true feelings, or hide resent-
ments/my face says it all.

My genes, shrouded by clay, and time, and
silence/unspoken words that say a lot about
what is true and what is not/there's humor
in the absurd, but only in retrospect/half-
heard whispers tease, threaten, cajole me
on despite their moans/try as they might to
stay my pen/ I blunder on/out of my depth/
to write it down before my death, and pass
the baton on.

My maternal Aunt and Uncles circa 1930

THE MAIDEN VOYAGE OF HMS PATIA

He was 19, a virgin, an orphan, naive.
He joined up because it was the right thing to do—and because he was alone.
Basic training completed, he was assigned a ship,
HMS Patia, a steel screw steamer.
Ship refitted, ready for action.
He trained, ready to kill.
They set sail, ready for adventure, to do their bit.
Half the crewman aged thirty and younger.
Dragged up, then called up—set off on their first and only mission.
Most don't die from drowning, he said.
They swallow the oil,
Or it gets in their lungs,
Or, they roast in the burning fuel.
This is what he remembers.

He hid his real self;
His heroism, the pain from the shrapnel wounds,
His intellect.
His lies and half truths,
His absences, his cold heart.
This is what I remember.

Not sure now, what else there was, or could have been.

**Albert Sadler RN, Volunteered,
28th September 1940**

Information:

HMS Patia, a merchant vessel completed in March 1922, was requisitioned by the Admiralty in September 1940. She was fitted out as fighter catapult ship. She was bombed and sunk by German He 111-bombers near 20G Buoy, Coquet Island, Northumberland, U.K on the 27th April, 1941, on her maiden voyage.

About 40 people were killed, including her Commander.

Before foundering her gunners managed to shoot down the attacking aircraft.

HE MAKES HER TOAST

My earliest memory?
Being in bed with my mother.
I remember I feel warm, and loved, and special.

My father is hovering at the bedroom door.
Home rarely, but jealous of me when he is.
He's home from sea, wants Mother to himself.
He brings her tea, resents my presence.

She wears the perfume he brought her from Paris. He makes her toast…but none for me.

MY GRANDMA'S HOUSE

This is what I remember:
My grandad reading to me,

The rhythmic thrum of a sewing machine,
And love served up as meat and two veg.

I hated the outside toilet,
Cold feet and chilblains,
And the threatening smell of carbolic soap.

Oh, how I wish I could have stayed there forever.

My granny, Mary Annie Smith circa 1940

THE MEMORIES I NEVER HAD

When I left, the Vale of York rolled up my years of quiet innocence
And stored them on a shelf marked 'Home' —
Just out of reach,
And so, I am forever incomplete.
Now I stride York's City walls,
As any other stranger can,
And contemplate the nakedness of not belonging
Like the rest, who haunt my past.
The history, the times of those long dead, invade my now.
A hidden hoard of secrets, sad regret, and loneliness revealed,
To trip me up, and scar my heart,
And bring to mind thoughts that were lost.
Dust and bones are all that's left of those who made, but knew me not.
Shadowed icons, laid prostrate, on purple altars of neglect —
No heroes here to celebrate.
Possessed by phantoms' DNA,
I step the stones, where once they trod.
And whisper names to unmarked graves,
And mourn the memories I never had.

Clifford's Tower, City of York, UK

Photo Anne Saddler ©2020

LETTER TO MY GRANNY

Dear Granny,

Today is Sunday, and I thought about you again. I think about you often.

Today is Sunday, and I remembered how you used to take me with you to church. We walked of course. You held my hand to keep me safe, and in your other hand you clutched your little Book of Common Prayer. I can see it now, red, and hard-backed. The print was so small it was difficult to read and you had to hold it close to your face. I didn't know it then, but for you it was a book of ritual, of focus, a guide-book to mysteries way beyond your understanding.

One of those rituals was 'churching'. You said a baby wouldn't thrive unless mother and child were blessed after a safe delivery. You will be pleased to know I made sure both my girls were churched before I took them home from the hospital, and arranged the same for both my grandsons. You probably won't be surprised to hear the vicar said it was a ritual he was rarely asked to perform these days. He was pleased to do it though, said he might look to do more.

You loved a traditional service didn't you? Preferably High Church, and sung in Latin —that 'foreign language' as you called it — with candles and bells and incense. The incense always made me sneeze, it still does.

I remember the priest would cleanse the congregation by dipping a rosemary twig in Holy Water and flicking it as us. You would cross yourself feverishly whenever he prostrated himself on the floor, in front of the altar.

The mystery of it all intrigued you. I think you thought it some kind of magic. You'd learned the 'old ways' from your mother, and those ideas were hard to let go of. Your superstitions never left you.

You always said you wished you were born a Roman Catholic. You never explained why. You liked everything Irish. You celebrated St Patrick's Day, wore green and got tipsy on cheap sherry. It was the highlight of your year.

You'll be pleased to hear that I continued to go to Sunday school, I even attended Confirmation Classes but, in the end I couldn't go through with it…couldn't commit. I didn't possess your faith you see and, to pretend I did, just didn't sit well.

I still have the bible you gave me at my baptism. I haven't opened it in years but I am comforted by the knowledge that you are still inside its pages. Your lovely inscription written in copperplate hasn't faded one bit.

Do you remember, Granny? When I was small and frightened you told me I had a Guardian Angel, someone special to watch over me, keep me safe —everyone had one you said. I was sure I saw him once, kneeling by my bed bathed in a golden light. My angel would always be at my side you said, would always love me, and protect me, as well as those I loved the best. Granny, you were wrong, where was he when I needed him?

You said God could see and hear me, knew what was best for me. He would guide me and look out for me if I was good, and loyal, and obedient. He knew my worth you said, He would answer all my prayers. It saddens me to tell you, Granny but, you were wrong.

You may be shocked to hear that God and I are no longer on speaking terms, but it doesn't seem to make much difference to my life. Actually, when I think about it, it was always me doing the talking anyway. And, if I'm honest, if He had answered back I think I would've freaked out. Now, I prefer your mother's ways. You'll be pleased to hear I don't waste my cursing energy. I use it wisely.

Granny, it's been a long time since we communicated. I hope that if you could see me now you'd feel a little pride in all I am, and all I have achieved in my life, despite the fact you said you preferred the boys.

I've done the best with the tools I've been given, just as you taught me to do, and I remember you always with affection.

Lots of love, your dutiful granddaughter, XXX

HAIKU CHAIN: FOR LOST CHILDREN

olivine pond frogs
spawned in a stagnant puddle
black tadpoles teeming

  jewelled kingfisher
  sharp eyed and rapier quick
  ashes and fishes

    orange and red leaves
    dance like drunken butterflies
    to autumn's largo

      pendulous spiders
        weaving silver-laced webbing
        frosted by snowflakes

my belly is fat, and full with our heart's delight , a gift of our love

      a winter snowdrop
      sterile unable to bloom
        sweet (still)born baby.

  brackish the water
  dirty yellow the spring gorse
  my heart is breaking

 no warmth in June's sun
 no joy in summer's long days
 no consolation

red and orange leaves
tumble and are crushed afoot
as autumn laments.

The author, aged one, with her mother

OTHER MATTERS

SHE HAD BLUE HAIR

I watched her as she spoke.

She had blue hair, badly dyed.

Blue hair suits no-one I thought.

She said, once, she lived in a wheelie-bin.

I didn't believe her.

She loved the attention, played on it,

Dropped in nuggets of information,

Enough to keep them intrigued but without any real context.

I spoke about something I knew to be true.

She contradicted, said she believed it wasn't so.

How irritating!

She had the power of youth, and gall, and tall-tales, and blue hair, and the funding no-one will give me.

I'm not a minority.

LOVE POEM TO A 21ST CENTURY WOMAN

I love you, I said,
To your shiny nourished hair, curled, hydrated — volumised to lift your roots,
Dyed in Auburn Russet, and cut and styled by Josh.

I love you, I said,
To your stunning sweeping eyebrows, sienna tinted, and Micro-bladed for fullness and symmetry, to frame your soft-thread lifted face.

I love you, I said,
To your eyes, made sensuous by sea-blue contacts and Sultry, by the clever use of shading, and natural layered lashes.

I love you, I said,
To your porcelain-capped teeth, and luscious lips plump with dermal-filler,
Welcoming my tongue in a stabilised shade of Fuchsia Pink cosmeceutical lipstick.

I love you, I said,
To your re-shaped nose and belly-button, and your newly tightened labia,
All pierced with gold and exquisite lab-grown diamonds.

I love you I said,
To your tasty, pert breasts, sized perfectly to fit my cupped hands,
And peachy butt, sculpted with the latest, safest, silicone implants.

I love you, I said.

I love your polished skin, your glowing, sun-kissed look, your acrylic French manicure, your Hollywood, your botoxed forehead and, of course, your career as an important influencer/vlogger.

I love you babe,
And you know I will—until I can afford a newer, fitter model…but, 'til then, let's just believe, we're soul mates on a journey to forever.

THE PHOTOGRAPH

I carry you in my pocket to all our favourite places,
The soft, salt breeze on my face, your tender kisses.

I carry you in my arms
Heavy, as I do the jobs you used to do.

I carry you in my eyes,
I see your face in the baby's.

And I see you in our children,
You're alive in the young ones.

I carry you in my memories,
Everything reminds me of you.

I carry you in my wishes,
But wishes are just thoughts,

And I carry you in my thoughts,
If only thoughts were real…

I carry you in my dreams,
There, I can talk to you as if you were here.

I carry you into my future,
I can do that because of our past.

I carry you in my heart,
Parted; but never apart.

I carry you in my pocket.

The Conversation: Two Lovers Parted By Death

I can feel your pain, he said.
I can see the terror in your eyes.

Why him? You ask.
Why not?
Death is life's only certainty.

I tell you this, she said.
The poets, clever though they are,
Can't word-paint a picture with the
dirty colours of my grief.

Celtic Cross photo by Anne Saddler

THE DEATH OF BEAUTY

Gunnera in autumn photo by Anne Saddler

In my dream, Beauty is filled with fragrance.
His scent is borne on the whiff of a breeze, soft against my warmed skin.

This place is silent.
Not morose or sad, nor a silence imposed for control or punishment.
It is silent because of its beauty.
There are no words to describe it.
Best then, to be mute, to gawp, to wander open-mouthed, in awe at beautifulness beyond all reasoning.

I feel ugly in this place.
I am ugly here.
I can feel my ugliness awakening.
It is set deep, and is burned into my soul.
I have to breathe hard and long;
I have to be strong, to keep my ugliness in check, repressed, unable to do harm.

Ugly is jealous. Ugly is cruel and vindictive. Ugly destroys.
Ugly will kill Beauty with a mere glance. A look of contempt will wither Beauty in a second.
Sweet air becomes fecund as Ugly spews dark filth into the sky.
Loveliness suffocates as dark thoughts threaten the brittle sunlight of ideas.

Ugly turns fragrance to odour and stench as she parades amongst Beauty, radiating her sullen disapproval.
'Ha,' she says. 'I see you Beauty, I know what you're hiding. I know you better than I know myself.'

And Beauty, generous kind Beauty, offers Ugly his gifts.
Multi-faceted flowers, their petals fashioned and shaped with love and care. His sunlight, and soft rain, his birdsong, and his rainbows.

And Ugly reaches out her hand, her long fingers trembling with anticipation. She desires Beauty, caresses Beauty, she wants to feel beautiful. But — her breath is foul, her thoughts dark and uncontrolled.
Her belly, full with the worms of worry and doubt, keep her nauseous and thin.

Ugly's sticky hands leave imprints wherever she goes.
Grimy reminders of her frequent and unwelcome visits.

Beauty's lips are full, and pink, and smile at simple pleasures.
Ugly's lips are eaten away by lies, and deceit, and treachery.
Beauty is mindful.
Ugly is chaotic.

And, when Ugly has played with Beauty long enough, Ugly opens her wings of despair and despond, and swallows Beauty's pride and self-worth.
And as Ugly flashes her stink-eye, and her shadow falls across Beauty's line of sight, Beauty says, 'No more Ugliness: I can take no more.'

And he flings himself off the bridge of despair and self-loathing into the canyon of guilt and blame. And his cry echoes into the empty chambers of Ugly's heads and hearts. And all Beauty is, passes into nothingness — except, and here is the secret, here is what Beauty knows and Ugly is ignorant of.

> Beauty's suicide scars the temporal
> horizon, it alters the time-line.

And, so it goes on, the war against waste, and hatred, and bigotry, and cruelty,

And everything that defines Ugly, with her eyes as blue as her melancholia.

> And, as the sun sets, and bleeds into tomorrow,
> Hope rises, and turns her head to the light.

❖ ❖ ❖

photo by Anne Saddler

❖ ❖ ❖

VINCENT'S IRISES

If your mind was tormented it did not show
In that portrait of flowers
With pigments that glow
On a canvas attacked with such masterly strokes.
Rich colour on colour
The image evokes
A place that was tranquil, a view to enjoy
As your innate skills
You began to employ.
The scene came alive as the paint left your brushes,
That snatched at the violet to form your irises.

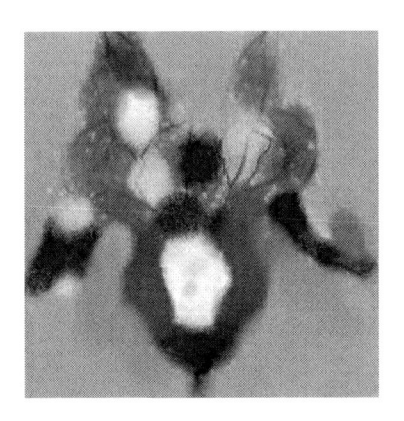

Iris iPad art by Anne Saddler

❖ ❖ ❖

THE SWORD OF TRUTH

The Sword of Truth in a religious hand
Is a portent of hell and damnation
Abide by the rules and fear ye the Lord
Or the consequence is your destruction.
Thump on the Bible; shout out the Word.
Be dogmatic, devout and be true
For the words of the Prophets,
Jehovah has spoken, and must be adhered to by you.

The Sword of Truth in a zealous hand
Is wielded and stands for a cause.
No compromise here, you will learn through your fear
That it's my way or no way at all
My ears will not hear, my eyes will not see,
I am closed to debate and discussion.

God's Word is my armour, His sword is my torch.
To get you to follow, my mission.

The Sword of Truth in a pious hand
Points to guilt, hypocrisy, shame.
I cannot sin; I have God within,
No-one's as devoted, as I am.
You'll see me on Sunday, but not when you're hungry,
I'll tithe but I won't give my time.
Jesus my Saviour, Hallelujah! I praise you!
Amen, the glory's all mine.

The Sword of Truth in an atheist's hand
Is a blade of pure steel, nothing more.
God is a myth, He doesn't exist,
He's the patron of hatred and war.
Free-thought is the way of the sceptic, I say.
Show courage, reject superstition
In your heart and your mind the Truth you will find.
Your faith is a farce, mere delusion.

The Sword of Truth in spiritual hands
Regardless of faith or conviction
Is a weapon so rare, so precious and fair,
It's a double edged sword of perfection.
The Truth is not doctrine, nor dogma, nor creed,
Not words on a page or from pulpit.
It's an abstract, etheric, incarnate, divine,
The Truth is your Truth and it needn't be mine.

What good is a body, bereft of a soul?
What good is a heart without spirit?

The sword is the Lord, and the book is the Word
And your life is his living sermon.

❖ ❖ ❖

MEGALITH

They stand,
A signal to the future.
'Look. We were here. Do not forget us.'
Still-life in a sunset of lost dreams.

Echoes of being.

Symbols of resourcefulness, and wisdom.
Otherworldly.
Solid, yet ethereal.
Dead objects opening the door to imaginings,
To the telling of stories.

Once upon a time, or perhaps, tomorrow…

Stonehenge, iPad art by Anne Saddler

❖ ❖ ❖

THE ARGUMENT

Hers is a disturbed experience of conversation.
The bitter sentences repeated, heard and evaluated,
Each word to another.

A momentary pause.

The hemlock words again repeated repeatedly, until the end.
To start again.
The intention to confuse, and in the confusion to slip away,
with pride intact.

Stop. Stop thinking.
Stop. Stop speaking.

She repeats the words, the rolling syllables, the sentences that wound, until,
Finally tested,
He turns in one direction, and she, another.

❖ ❖ ❖

THE MISUNDERSTANDING

They rolled once, then twice.
However they landed,
She moved to where they were.

Something had blasted them,
She could not know it.
Something had moved them,
She could not know it.
Something had a dark ending.
She would not know it.

Update the shaken night.
Jump, reach for the dawning light.
They cry: Dreaming in the void.

Lighten the possibility of change in subtle ways,
Or, in a sudden wind.

Turn the page,
Open a door,
Move the barrier between us.

A fleeting joy,
How could she know it?

A ray of hopefulness,
How could she know it?

A memory of sadness,
Of course she knew it.

The promise given, and,
Harvesting what was no longer dead,
She moved to where they were.

◆ ◆ ◆

REDUNDANT

I stare through the rain-streaked window.
Everything is grey.
The low cloud dampens my mood, slows my mind.
I stay in bed.
Warm tea in my mug, warm dog nestled between my knees.
Nothing to get up for.

***

My witch-mother prophesied:
When a woman hits fifty, an invisible mantle descends from the ether to veil her…obscure her. Once cloaked, her light grows dim, her presence dwindles, she begins to fade into the background. Her presence diminished, she sinks slowly into obscurity.

> Believe me, she said. You'll see, she
> said. Mark my words, she said.

I watch the Gulls.
They swirl, and twirl, in the stilled, salted air.
Strangely silent, they wait for the cloud to lift.
They come each week; they know it's Tuesday.
Below the fog, dust-bins filled with promise,
Line the streets like rows of blackened teeth.
There's easy pickings to be had from rotting mouths.
If I were a gull, I'd get in there first, tear at the bags,
Make my chances, pick out The best.
I wouldn't share.
Playing nice doesn't get you anywhere.

***

My mother warned me. I didn't listen.
It'll be different for me, I thought.
I'm strong, work hard. I'm respected, admired.
I toe the line, give my best, they know my worth.
I'll shrug the cloak from my capable shoulders.
I'll brush the suffocating heaviness of 50 off, like dandruff.
These are my days, not yours…
Things have changed, Mother.

***

The fifth decade, the cursed benefactress of maturity;
Ambition blinded by age.

It's eyes put out by crow's feet, grey hairs, hot-flushes-in-important-meetings,
And the need to be in bed by 22:30.
Capability? No longer recognised.
Knowledge? Now largely ignored.
Opinions? Un-sought, or worse, unwelcome.
Aspirations? Side-lined for new projects.
Ambition? Over-looked for new jobs — no promotion.

"Hello? Hello? Can no-body see me?"

***

Nature sticks the knife in deeper…and twists.
The comfy nest flown without a backward glance.
Looks compromised by bleeding lipstick,
Flats instead of heels,
Used-up hormones. Cob-web brain.
The dis-in-ter-est-ed partner.

***

White and cream houses dot the
far side of the valley.
They hover on a marshmallow of
pinky-grey sea mist,
Empty shells with no souls.
Their occupants left for work an hour ago.
A busy commute, a full diary.
Compliant automatons on their daily grind.
I wonder if, like me, someone across
the valley is lying in bed,
Abandoned, with warm tea, and
a dog, and no future.

***

I think about the day ahead — there's no reason to stir.
I inherited my mother's cloak, and disappeared along with my successes.
I've nothing to do, no-one to see.
No In-box now I'm out.

Purposeless, worthless, pointless, redundant,
I'm useless; of-no-use.
May as well stay here then…in bed,
With warm tea in my mug, and warm dog nestled between my knees.
I stare through the rain-streaked window,
And everything is grey.

◆ ◆ ◆

ABOUT THE AUTHOR

Anne Saddler

Anne lives in a lively Cornish port in the South West of England with her husband, and Ted the dog.

Anne writes poetry, essays, articles, and fiction, as well as memoir and art reviews.

Anne's second book, 'Tales From Walmgate: A Shocking Case of Felo-De-Se' will be released summer 2020. The book, a fusion of fiction and memoir, re-imagines the lives of her paternal ancestors, the Saddler family, who lived in the City of York during the reign of Queen Victoria.

Anne is a spoken word performer and recites her work in venues on her local literary scene.

Printed in Great Britain
by Amazon